SLY COOPER

by Michael Anthony Steele

SCHOLASTIC INC.

New York   Toronto   London   Auckland   Sydney
Mexico City   New Delhi   Hong Kong   Buenos Aires

No part of this work may be reproduced in whole or in part, or stored in a retrieval system, or transmitted in any form or by any means, electronic, mechanical, photocopying, recording, or otherwise, without written permission of the publisher. For information regarding permission, write to Scholastic Inc., Attention: Permissions Department, 557 Broadway, New York, NY 10012.

ISBN 0-439-82945-3

12 11 10 9 8 7 6 5 4 3 2 1   6 7 8 9 10/0

SLY COOPER

Sly Cooper dove under the short table. He tucked in his furry legs and pulled his long, ringed tail close to his body. The guard snorted and stopped in mid–stride, aiming his flashlight in Sly's direction. The beam washed over the table, but Sly was safely hidden. With a final snort, the guard continued down the dark hallway.

Sly squirmed out from under the table. He crouched low and snuck up behind the tall warthog guard, extending his long cane. Using the cane's hooklike handle, he carefully reached into the guard's back pocket. With amazing speed and skill, Sly pulled out a small brass key. The guard continued on his patrol, unaware of what was going on behind him. With the key safely in his leg pack and the guard out of sight, Sly continued on his mission. He ran up the nearby stairs to the top floor of the building.

Sly Cooper was no ordinary thief; he was a *master* thief. In fact, he came from a long line of master thieves, which meant he stole only from *master* criminals. That's why Sly Cooper stole only from the biggest criminals in the world. He was very good at it. In fact, he was the best.

Sly reached the top of the stairs. He slowly poked his head into the dimly lit hallway. Tall bookshelves lined the corridor, and chandeliers hung from the ceiling. Shafts of moonlight poured through a few small windows along the exterior wall. Oddly, there were no guards patrolling this level.

This is too easy, Sly thought.

He stepped into the moonlight and

crept down the hall. As he traveled, the door at the opposite end of the corridor came into view. That was his goal — Dimitri's office.

Dimitri was a former art student turned art forger. His goons often stole priceless works of art from all over the world. Then Dimitri's forgers would copy them, and the lanky lizard quickly made a small fortune selling the fake fine art. With his riches, he had built several nightclubs all over the world, making him an underworld celebrity.

Sly had recently learned that the lizard had stolen another priceless piece. The raccoon was going to relieve Dimitri of the terrible burden of ownership.

Unfortunately, the master thief soon realized *why* no guards patrolled this level. He halted in front of several thin security beams. The crimson lasers criss-crossed the floor in front of him. There were so many of them, there was no way he could merely step over them. He had to find another way.

"I always like a challenge," Sly said to himself.

He adjusted his hat and sprung into the air, performing a midair somersault and hooking his cane on to one of the chandeliers. As he dangled above the security beams, he swung back and forth, gaining momentum. Then he unhooked himself and soared from the first chandelier to the next one. Gaining more momentum, he swung to the next one, and then on to the next. When he came to the last chandelier, he saw that the door was still too far away. If he leaped off the swinging light fixture, he wouldn't make it. He'd hit the security beams and set off the alarm.

Sly spun to his left and rocked toward the nearby bookcase. He leaped off the chandelier and landed on the top shelf. The bookcase creaked under his weight, but it held. With his back to the wall, he shuffled toward the end of the hallway.

As Sly neared his goal, he heard a clinking sound. He craned his neck and saw a glass bottle one shelf below. It wobbled back and forth with each step he took. Sly knew this was no ordinary bottle; it was a clue bottle. He could tell by the scrap of paper jutting from its mouth. With one fluid motion, Sly swung his cane and broke the bottle. Then he quickly snatched up the paper with his other hand.

He examined his find. Several numbers and letters were printed across the small scrap. To anyone else, it would have looked like gibberish. In fact, to Sly Cooper it looked like gibberish. However, he knew that it was really a secret code. He also knew that criminals didn't trust anyone, especially themselves. Most of the major ones hid clue bottles around their lairs. The bottles contained pieces of a code. Once all the pieces were put together and analyzed, they usually revealed something important. Of course, Sly wasn't able to decipher the code. He specialized in thievery, not code breaking. But he did know someone who could break the code.

Sly reached into his leg pack and whipped out his binocucom — binoculars and a communications device all in one. He held the device up to his eyes and pressed the power button. A small turtle with thick glasses squinted back at him in the tiny view screen.

"I found the last bottle, Bentley," Sly announced.

"That's perfect," replied Bentley. "Transmit the contents and I'll decipher the code." Sly typed in the seemingly random letters and numbers. No sooner had he finished typing when Bentley cracked the code. "It's the combination to Dimitri's safe," he announced. "Three . . . Eight . . . Five!"

"Perfect," said Sly. "Have Murray start the van. This job is almost over!"

Murray's face appeared in the

opposite view screen. The pink hippo adjusted his goggles. "Don't worry, Sly," he said. "*The Murray* is ready to put the pedal to the metal!"

Sly chuckled as he turned off his binocucom and returned it to his pack. Then he carefully slid to the end of the bookcase. He leaped into the air, flipped, and landed in front of Dimitri's office door. Using the key he had snatched from the guard, he unlocked the door and pushed it open.

Sly leaped through the door and landed in a crouch. He glanced around, making sure he was alone. He was. His prize stood directly in front of him. Resting on a large easel was a painting of a lizard with long black hair. Her eyes met Sly's and a hint of a smile touched the corners of her mouth. It was Leo Rhino's famous painting, the Mona Lizard.

Sly knew he would find it here. He knew Dimitri liked to gaze upon his newly stolen paintings before copying them and selling the well-crafted forgeries.

Sly grabbed the painting and moved toward his bonus prize — Dimitri's safe. He entered the combination and popped it open. Inside, he found a very interesting piece of paper. He folded it up and placed it in his pack. In its place, he left his famous calling card — a tiny card cutout of a masked raccoon.

With the painting securely under one arm, Sly opened the office window. He had one foot out when her heard a commotion. Two guards ran through the office door. They raced toward him with their clubs in the air. He must have set off a silent alarm when he opened the safe!

"I'd like to stay and play," Sly said as he climbed out onto the fire escape. "But I have a party to go to!"

The guards reached through the window and swung their clubs at him. He easily ducked them and leaped into the cool night air. He hooked a drainpipe with his cane and slid safely to the ground. Then he jumped into the back of the waiting van and closed the door.

"Punch it, Murray!" Sly ordered.

"Taste the speed!" Murray shouted. Sly flew back as the van rocketed forward.

"Was the mission a success?" asked Bentley.

"And then some," Sly replied. He reached into his pouch and pulled out the scrap of paper, handing it to Bentley.

Bentley adjusted his glasses and squinted through the thick lenses. "An invitation?"

"That's right," said Sly. "Pack your bags, boys. We're going to Monaco!"

CHAPTER 2

"Where are you, Sly Cooper?" wondered Inspector Carmelita Montoya Fox. "Where will you strike next?"

The Interpol inspector blew a strand of curly dark hair from her face. She stared at the bulletin board over her desk. The faces of Sly, Bentley, and Murray stared back at her. Their photographs were pinned atop a large map. Red circles marked all the locations the Cooper clan had hit since they had defeated the Fiendish Five, a band of well-known thieves. Carmelita thought the sneaky raccoon would have taken a vacation after that particular adventure. After all, he and his crew had defeated five of the biggest names in crime. On top of that, they had been able to slip through her fingers once again. But Sly Cooper had been quite busy since then.

Carmelita focused her gaze on the photo of Sly himself. In the picture, as in real life, the bandit wore an arrogant smirk. Inspector Fox knew the raccoon thought himself to be a master thief, but she thought otherwise. Just because Sly and his cohorts stole from criminals didn't make them anything special. Thieves were thieves in her book, no matter who they stole from or how cute they were. In Inspector Fox's mind, Cooper belonged behind bars, and Carmelita believed she was just the fox for the job of putting him there.

Her long bushy tail swished as she paced back and forth in her office. She had to come up with a way to get ahead of Sly. Sometimes he and his crew worked in predictable patterns. In the past, when Sly had been after big criminals, Carmelita always had some idea as to where he might turn up next. Now, he could be anywhere. She stopped her pacing and stared, once again, into the raccoon's big brown eyes. She wished she knew where he planned to strike next. She wished she had some kind of edge.

There was a light knock at the door.

"Come in," Carmelita said without taking her eyes from Cooper's photograph.

"Uh, excuse me, Inspector Fox," said Detective Winthorp. "I have something for you."

"Now's not a good time, Winthorp," Carmelita said as she put on her glasses. She leaned forward to get a closer look.

"I think . . . I hope . . . you'll find this interesting," Winthorp replied.

Carmelita sighed and spun to face him. The short weasel held a wilting red rose in one hand. "That?" she asked. "A droopy rose?"

Winthorp's cheeks turned as red as

his bow tie. "What, this?" He looked at the rose, then tossed it away. "No, of course not."

"Then what is it?" she asked, annoyed by his interruption.

Winthorp reached into his pocket and pulled out a small envelope. "You wanted me to keep tabs on big names in the crime world, right?" He handed the envelope to Inspector Fox. "I think this counts."

Carmelita opened the envelope and pulled out an engraved invitation. It was for an engagement party. It seemed Dimitri had decided to marry Madame D'Oinkeau, and he was throwing a party at her mansion in Monaco to celebrate.

Carmelita didn't think Dimitri was the type to settle down and start a family. However, she did know D'Oinkeau's large smuggling operation could come in handy for an art forger like Dimitri. Then Carmelita noticed the bottom of the invitation. "Witness the Madame's generous engagement gift to Dimitri — the world-famous statue, the Venus de Whalo."

A wide grin stretched across Carmelita's face. *Now* she knew why Dimitri was marrying D'Oinkeau — or at least why he was becoming engaged to her. The inspector smiled for another reason. She knew that Sly Cooper wouldn't be able to resist such a prize. He was bound to try to steal the famous statue. Inspector Fox wasn't about to miss this engagement party.

CHAPTER 3

Sly Cooper leaped from the balcony of the safe house. He soared through the warm night air and landed on a nearby rooftop. Then he dashed across the roof and dove off the other side. He latched on to the drainpipe of yet another building and climbed upward. When he reached the top, he ran along a thin cable leading to a tall tower. Once atop the tower, Sly leaped onto its narrow spire. Balancing on the sharp point, he surveyed his surroundings.

The city of Monaco was buzzing with nightlife, its citizens chatting happily as they strolled to and from restaurants, nightclubs, and parties. Their cheery voices blended with soft music and crept up to the rooftops. Sly was on his way to a party himself. However, he was an uninvited guest, and he wouldn't be staying for long.

He pulled out his binocucom and aimed it at a tall mansion two blocks away. Surrounded by palm trees, the large building towered over the exotic city. Its large pillars sparkled and its tiled roof gleamed. *Dimitri certainly knows how to live the good life,* Sly thought to himself.

Sly pressed a button, and the binocucom zoomed in on the structure. Bentley's face appeared in the tiny view screen. "Well, Sly, if you like big, mean, warthog guards, then you're in luck," said the turtle. "The grounds are crawling with them!"

Sly aimed the binocucom at the top of the mansion. "Then I'll go in through the roof." He focused on a large skylight. Zooming closer, he zeroed in on a padlock dangling from the hinged window.

"That's a good idea," Bentley agreed.

"But you'll need to pickpocket the key from Dimitri's head of security."

"Not a problem," Sly replied. "Wouldn't be a master thief if I didn't know how to pick someone's pocket."

"Unless my math is wrong — and my math is never wrong — he should be walking around the corner right about . . . now," said Bentley.

Sly aimed the binocucom at the street below. A warthog wearing a blue security uniform came into view. "I see him," Sly replied.

Murray's face appeared in the opposite view screen. "Hey, Sly. Do you want me to give that guard a taste of my Thunder Flop?" The hippo grinned. "It knows neither friend nor foe, only destruction!"

Sly chuckled. "No, thanks, pal. I think we're going for stealth on this mission."

"Good luck, Sly," said Bentley. He adjusted his thick glasses. "Remember, you can count on me to be your eyes and ears."

"Wouldn't have it any other way," Sly said with a smile.

The master thief turned off the binocucom and shoved it back into his pouch. Then he leaped off the spire and landed on a thin cable. He bent low as he slid down the wire toward the ground below.

◆   ◆   ◆

Sly Cooper never did a job without Bentley and Murray. They were the best crew in the entire world. They were also the closest thing to a family he had. Sly's father had been taken from him when he was very young, landing the little raccoon in the Happy Camper Orphanage. There he met a very young Murray and an equally young Bentley. The three of them quickly became friends.

It wasn't long before they planned their first job together. The orphanage's headmistress, Ms. Puffin, wasn't a master criminal. But she was a mean old bird who stole all of the kids' holiday cookies. That made her criminal enough for Sly and his friends. Using crayons, rulers, and glue, young Bentley quickly came up with a master plan. They were going to steal back those cookies.

Back in Monaco, Sly neared the bottom of his steep slide. He leaped from the cable and flew toward a large awning. He bounced off the awning and landed on the roof of a short building. Below him, the head of security paced along the sidewalk. Other pedestrians bustled around him.

"The sidewalk is too crowded right now," Bentley's voice buzzed in Sly's earpiece. "You'll have to wait for just the right moment to move in."

"Good idea, Bentley," Sly whispered back. "Dimitri's party needs to be the only spectacle of the evening."

He continued to creep along the

rooftop. Unfortunately, he didn't see the loose tile just in front of him. As his foot came down on it, the tile slid out from under him. It flew off the roof and sailed right toward Dimitri's head of security!

CHAPTER 4

Inspector Carmelita Montoya Fox enjoyed a good stakeout. Many officers thought they were boring assignments. They thought stakeouts were nothing more than long hours with bad food. However, Carmelita enjoyed setting the trap. She relished the anticipation of the crook's arrival. And nothing beat actually springing the trap itself. A good stakeout was the backbone of police work. This, however, was not a good stakeout.

Carmelita was uncomfortable in her long evening gown. She was much more at ease in her usual attire — her leather jacket, trousers, and tall boots. The inspector felt even more awkward being surrounded by Monaco's high society. And to top it off, she had to listen to the boring ramblings of Dimitri's fiancée, Madame D'Oinkeau.

She stood in the grand ballroom of her Monaco mansion. The lizard's engagement party was in full swing. It was packed with the richest snobs Monaco had to offer — a fact that Madame D'Oinkeau was proud to point out.

"Look at this party, Dimitri," Madame D'Oinkeau gushed to her husband-to-be. "It's like we own Monaco. Anyone who is anyone is here!"

The purple lizard put an arm around his portly fiancée. "The world is taken by our storm!"

Carmelita stifled a small laugh. Dimitri always dressed in ridiculous nightclub garb, like brightly colored shirts and ultra-wide collars and flashy jewelry. He also usually tried to act "cool" by using hip lingo and catchphrases. To Carmelita's amusement, he often got them wrong.

"You can dig that and take it straight to da bank," Dimitri added.

D'Oinkeau grabbed Dimitri's chin and rubbed her wide snout against his nose. "Of course, my snookems!"

Carmelita wasn't sure, but she thought she saw a hint of revulsion in Dimitri's eyes. If so, it would confirm her suspicions. She was sure that the slimy lizard was marrying the snooty Madame for her money. Carmelita didn't put anything past Dimitri. In fact, if she had enough evidence, she would lock them both up tonight. Dimitri would be arrested for his illegal forging activities, and D'Oinkeau for her smuggling operation.

The Madame grabbed Carmelita's arm. "Come, Inspector," she said. "I want to show you why I'm particularly glad you came this evening."

The short pig led Carmelita down a nearby hallway. Dimitri followed closely behind. Along the way, they passed several paintings on the wall, and sculptures on pedestals.

"Don't you just love Dimitri's most glorious art collection?" D'Oinkeau asked. She didn't wait for an answer. "Yes, money can buy the best of things," she continued.

They came upon an open room. More paintings lined the walls, and a large sculpture stood in the center. It was probably the most tasteless work of art Carmelita had ever seen.

"This is what I wanted to show you," D'Oinkeau continued. "Allow me to introduce you to the world's most valuable engagement gift — the Venus de Whalo!"

"I'm . . . I'm . . . speechless," stammered Carmelita. And she was. Of course, she knew the statue was there; that's why she had come. She knew Sly Cooper couldn't resist stealing such a valuable prize from a criminal like Dimitri. However, Carmelita wasn't ready for the pure tastelessness of the piece.

The statue was of a large whale standing upright on its tail. Wrapped in a toga, the whale smiled at whomever fell under its gaze. Carmelita didn't know why something like that was so valuable. Then again, she was in law enforcement, not in the arts.

"This statue means the world to me," D'Oinkeau added. "Surely it will be safe with you here. Won't it, Inspector?"

Carmelita smiled. "Tonight is a night of celebration, Madame D'Oinkeau. Your statue is safe with me."

She turned back to the hideous sculpture and grimaced. She hoped she was right about Cooper. She hoped she wouldn't have to stare at the ugly statue all night for nothing.

CHAPTER 5

The warthog guard bent over just in time. The loose tile sailed over his head and smashed onto the street beside him. Startled, the security guard turned toward where the tile had landed. Then he went off to investigate.

Sly smiled. *Whew!* he thought. *That was a close one.*

Sly kept pace by tiptoeing along the edge of the roof. This time, he was more careful about where he stepped.

The master thief paused and looked up and down the walkway. He frowned. The evening pedestrians didn't show any signs of thinning. He would never get his chance to pick the guard's pocket.

Just then, the security chief took a sharp right down a dark alley. The large warthog snorted as he turned on a flashlight. Sly knew this was his chance. He leaped off the building and silently dropped behind the guard. The warthog cocked his head as if he heard something. Sly turned his cane over in his hands. If the guard turned and saw him, it would be either fight or flight. Since Sly really needed that key, it would have to be fight.

The guard snorted once more and then continued down the dark alley. With cautious steps, Sly crept up behind him. He carefully extended his cane, gently dipping the handle into the guard's back pocket to snatch the key. Sly froze and let the large warthog continue to lumber down the alley.

With the key safely stashed in his leg pouch, Sly hooked his cane on to a lamppost. He climbed up the post and back onto the roof of the short building. He dashed across the roof toward Dimitri's mansion. When he reached the edge of the roof, he launched himself into the air, soaring toward the taller building. At the last second, Sly extended his cane and latched on to a drainpipe. Then he placed the cane in his mouth and grabbed on with both hands. He quickly scrambled up the pipe toward the roof.

Sly peeked past the roofline. Unfortunately, one of Dimitri's servants stood beside the skylight. The gecko must have come onto the roof for some fresh air. Sly had battled these types of goons in the past. They weren't very tough, but they could certainly sound the alarm. One shout and the entire mission could be ruined. Sly would have to take this guy out as quietly as possible.

Luckily, the gecko faced the other way. Sly silently hurdled over the edge. Keeping low, he crept up behind his opponent. Sly decided to use his special silent obliteration move. Using his cane, he lifted the gecko into the air. While the goon was still above his head, Sly grabbed him with the hook of his cane. Sly spun around and dropped the gecko to the ground. He was out cold.

Sly glanced around. At last, the top of Dimitri's mansion appeared to be free of both guards and servants. The master thief darted toward the large skylight. Crouching beside it, Sly whipped out the key and unlocked the padlock.

"Dimitri, you may be rich but you're not too bright," Sly whispered to himself. "Putting all your guards on the ground means there's no one left to guard the roof."

Sly slowly opened the skylight and peered inside. The dark hallway below seemed to be deserted. Using well-practiced stealth, Sly dropped through the opening. His cane at the ready, he looked around for more guards.

"Good work, Sly," buzzed Bentley's

voice. "Now you'll need to find the ventilation maintenance room, just like we planned."

"No problem," Sly replied. He slowly moved down the hallway. "But it wouldn't hurt to pick up a few more treasures along the way."

"Now wait a minute, Sly," said Bentley. "I don't think it's a good idea to stray from the plan."

Sly moved toward a closed door. "What's the fun of being a thief if you can't snoop around a bit?" He reached toward the doorknob.

"But what about the plan?" asked Bentley.

Sly opened the door and got a big surprise. Three very large warthogs looked up from what they were doing.

"I think we need a plan B," replied Sly.

CHAPTER 6

"For security guards, you guys sure have a strange sense of style," Sly said.

The ugly warthogs each held a paintbrush and sat in front of unfinished paintings. Their work matched photographs of different paintings on the wall. These warthogs were Dimitri's art forgers, and they were copying the originals.

"He's seen us," snorted one of the warthogs. "Get him, boys!"

The three beasts dropped their brushes and charged toward Sly. The nimble raccoon leaped over the goons, flipped, and landed behind them.

"You're not playing very nice, boys."

Sly chuckled. "Forging fine art? Now that's low."

Sly swung his cane and cracked the closest warthog on the head. *BAM!* Then he hooked him with the cane's handle and flung him across the room. *CRASH!*

Then one of the other fiends swung at Sly. The thief ducked under the meaty fist. Instead of hitting Sly, the warthog smacked his fellow art forger in the face. *Ka-POW!*

"Fist plus face equals pain," Sly joked. The two warthogs turned and growled at him. Sly merely shrugged. "Artists can be so sensitive."

The warthogs charged, and Sly turned and ran. He leaped atop a supply cabinet, just ahead of their grasping hands. Then the thief sprang off the top of the cabinet and flew backward toward the center of the room. He latched his cane on to a dangling hook and swung over the warthogs' heads. Sly pulled his legs in just out of their reach.

"Looks as if someone's been harboring some pent-up anger," Sly jabbed. He continued to swing in a wide arc around the room. "Why don't you let me help you release some of that rage?"

Sly swung back around and slammed both feet into the two warthogs. *SMACK!* They flew across the room and landed in a heap beside the first one. All three were out cold.

Sly unhooked his cane, backflipped, and landed gracefully on the floor. "All right, back to the schedule. I didn't come here to teach the ethics of art forgers."

Suddenly, a hulking figure barged into the room. The giant wore a security uniform and loped toward Sly. His two huge hands were raised above his head.

Before he knew it, Sly was swept up in those two powerful arms. He tried to squirm free, but it was no use.

"You're okay!" yelled Murray. "We were worried about you!" Sly could barely breathe as Murray squeezed him tighter.

"Okay, big guy," Sly grunted. "You can let go now."

Murray dropped him and Sly caught his breath. "What are you doing here?" he asked. "I can handle three measly little art forgers."

"When you called for a plan B, Bentley did what any good genius would do." The big pink hippo put his hands on his hips and puffed out his chest. "He sent in *The Murray*."

"Okay, that explains why you're here," said Sly. "But why the security guard outfit?"

Murray raised a chubby finger. "Ah, that's plan B!" He reached behind his back and pulled out another blue uniform.

Sly smiled.

CHAPTER 7

". . . And there it sat on display for several years," Madame D'Oinkeau droned on. "But due to some bad debts on the museum's part, I was able to *acquire* the wonderful piece for a very modest price. Of course, everyone knows that the Venus de Whalo is priceless, and the museum must have been desperate to sell it for so little!"

Inspector Fox stifled her twentieth yawn. "Oh, of course."

Madame D'Oinkeau leaned over and squeezed Dimitri's chin. "And I couldn't think of a better engagement gift to give to my precious Dimitri."

The lizard jerked a bit as if he were on the verge of falling asleep as well. Then he affectionately pinched one of her chubby cheeks. "It digs better den da biggest bling, my candy piece."

Carmelita rolled her eyes at the disgusting display of mock affection. It was obvious from Dimitri's behavior that he didn't really care about Madame D'Oinkeau. He was only marrying her so he could get his hands on the priceless statue. Carmelita wondered if she should tell D'Oinkeau. Then again, she doubted the love-struck pig would believe her.

Suddenly, two security guards ran into the room. One was very large and plump. The other was shorter and somewhat attractive.

"Mr. Dimitri!" shouted the shorter guard. "Madame Oinkeau! Excuse us, please!"

The Madame's face reddened. "It's *D'*Oinkeau," she huffed. "And what's the meaning of this intrusion?"

"There's been a security breach upstairs!" The smaller guard pointed back toward the large staircase. "An intruder has been apprehended. He's being held in the attic!"

Dimitri's eyes widened. "In da attic?"

"Yes, in the *attic*," the guard replied with a smile.

Carmelita squinted at the shorter guard. His hat was pulled low on his head. The brim obscured some of his face. Carmelita thought he looked slightly familiar, though she couldn't quite place him.

Dimitri stepped toward the guards. "Great work, my home boys," he said. The lizard turned to D'Oinkeau and Carmelita. His long tail swished nervously. "Let's kick it hard core, shall we? Da party is in the full swing!"

Carmelita leaned to the left to get a better look at the guard. Dimitri leaned in front of her. "Inspector, I insist," he said.

"Da situation is being dealt with proper. Now let's roll."

"Excuse me, ma'am," the guard interrupted. "The intruder fits the description of Sly Cooper."

Carmelita's eyes widened. "Cooper!" She ran toward the security guards, pushing past them and dashing toward the stairs.

"Inspector!" Dimitri called behind her. "It's very dangerous. You really should chill cool with da party!"

Carmelita sprinted up the staircase. She heard D'Oinkeau's labored breathing as she hurried up the stairs after her. "A real criminal," said D'Oinkeau. "How exciting!"

"Uh . . . I guess we both can't be flaking on da party," Dimitri stammered at the bottom of the staircase. "I'll . . . uh . . . best be checking just to see dat things are grooving."

"Always thinking, pumpkin," D'Oinkeau replied. "I'll see you soon."

Inspector Fox raced up three flights of stairs toward the attic. When she reached the top, she saw a closed door in front of her. As D'Oinkeau panted up behind her, Carmelita kicked open the door.

"I have you now, Cooper!" Inspector Fox shouted.

She charged into the room to find it torn apart. Broken canvases and easels were strewn everywhere. Ruptured paint tubes littered the floor, and paint was splattered all over everything. Several tattered photos of famous paintings hung from the walls. It looked suspiciously like what was left of a forging operation.

Madame D'Oinkeau gasped. "Dimitri, a forger?" she shrieked. "It can't be!"

"It sure seems that way," said Carmelita.

A raspy sound caught the inspector's attention. She turned to her left to see three unconscious warthogs. They were tied up and looked as if they had lost a fight. One was snoring very loudly.

D'Oinkeau knelt beside the warthogs. "But I thought they said Sly Cooper was tied up here."

"They did." Carmelita's eyes narrowed. "But it appears we've been led astray."

Suddenly, her eyes widened. She turned and darted out of the room.

"Where are you going, Inspector?" D'Oinkeau asked as she huffed after her, trying her best to keep up.

"To the statue!" Carmelita replied.

The inspector sprinted down the stairs and pushed through the crowded ballroom. Unsurprisingly, Dimitri was nowhere to be found. Unfortunately, when she entered the gallery, neither was the statue. The Venus de Whalo was gone!

In its place sat an all-too-familiar sight — a small blue card cut in the shape of a raccoon's head. Sly Cooper had stolen the statue.

"No!" Carmelita yelled. "That no-good, lowdown, rotten, lousy thief!"

CHAPTER 8

Sly stood on top of the van and pulled his cane as hard as he could. Its hooked handle was latched to the head of the Venus de Whalo. Murray grunted as the huge statue rested on his back. The hippo slowly backed toward the van as Sly guided it inside with his cane.

"My dad was right," said Sly. "You don't have a plan unless you have a plan B."

Murray huffed as he shoved the statue farther into the van. "I hope this plan B involves food. I'm starving!"

Sly thought back to their very first heist. His father's advice had been just as helpful then as it was now. Their plan B had come in handy that night as well.

⌐ ⌐ ⌐

Sly pictured himself back at the Happy Camper Orphanage. Bentley had come up with the perfect plan to steal back the cookies from Ms. Puffin. All the plan needed was a daring thief to pull it off. Young Sly Cooper was that daring thief.

Young Sly had snuck into Ms. Puffin's office earlier that day. He hid in the trash can until she departed for the night. When Ms. Puffin left and locked the door, he poked his head out of the crumpled papers, then he carefully crawled out of the can and tiptoed to the window. He pushed it open and a plastic cup flew inside. Sly caught it and ducked beneath the windowsill.

"Bentley, this is Sly," he spoke into the cup. "I'm in position one. Can you hear me? Over."

"Terrific!" said a voice from inside

the cup. "My ingenious cup-municator is working flawlessly." Sly held up the cup. A long string led from the cup and out the window. "Move to position two immediately," Bentley instructed from the other end of the cup-municator. "Operation Cookie Connection has begun!"

Sly rose and peaked out the window. He saw Bentley holding the other end of the cup-municator. The young turtle sat in a wagon full of electronic equipment he had made himself, using different parts from electronic toys.

Murray sat on a large tricked-out tricycle in front of the wagon. Bentley's wagon was tied to the back of the tricycle. The hippo had his feet firmly on the pedals. Even back then, Murray had been an eager getaway driver.

Sly turned his attention back to the office. He gazed up at the tall bookcase. A plump cookie jar sat at the very top, far out of reach. The young raccoon licked his lips and flicked his tail. He could almost taste those cookies. He quickly began to rearrange some of Ms. Puffin's furniture.

Bentley's plan was brilliant. He had calculated that the operation should take no more than three minutes and forty-two seconds. That was the average time between Ms. Puffin's leaving for the night and the arrival of Scary John, the janitor. They had planned and timed the caper perfectly. Sly's father would have been proud of them that night.

Sly placed a tall floor lamp next to the bookshelf. Then he pushed Ms. Puffin's desk toward the lamp. That wouldn't have been a problem for Sly Cooper, master thief. But for Sly Cooper, young orphan, it took a while. The desk seemed to merely crawl forward as Sly heaved with all his might.

When the desk was close enough, Sly jumped on top. Breathing hard, he picked up his end of the cup-municator. "Okay, Bentley. Everything is all set!"

"You don't have the cookies yet?!"

Bentley's voice asked, panic in his voice. "Abort mission! We've run out of time!"

Sly looked up at the cookie jar. He tightened his lips. He wasn't letting the prize get away. Sly got a running start and dove off the desk. A master thief must adapt and think on his feet, *he thought to himself.* He grabbed the hanging chain switch on the lamp. The light clicked on as his weight pulled it down. Sly swung his legs out and let go. Then he soared toward the top of the bookcase and grabbed the top shelf. His hands were inches away from the cookie jar.

Sly held on with one hand as he pulled out the plastic cup. "It's okay, Bentley," he said. "I'm almost at the cookies." Sly looked over his shoulder at the floor below. It was a long way down. He swallowed hard. "This didn't look so high from way down there."

"You're out of time!" Bentley shouted. "Get out while you still can!"

"Hold on, guys," Sly said as he pulled

himself onto the shelf. He took off his hat and wiped his brow.

He turned and removed the lid from the cookie jar. He reached in and grabbed a handful of cookies, then froze. There were footsteps outside. "I hear someone," he whispered into the cup. "Is that one of you guys?"

"No, we're both outside the window," Bentley replied.

Sly's eyes widened as he heard the sound of a key jiggling in the lock. "Then that must be Scary John, the janitor!"

CHAPTER 9

Terrified, young Sly Cooper sat on top of Ms. Puffin's bookshelf. He watched as the door's dead bolt spun with a loud CLICK. Then the doorknob began to turn. Sly didn't have time to climb down and jump out the window. He would be caught for sure.

"I'll save you, Sly!" Murray yelled from outside. "Just leave it to . . . The Murray!"

"Plan B!" Bentley's voice yelled from the plastic cup.

Sly had just put on his hat when he felt the cup-municator jerk in his hand. Luckily, he tightened his grip as the string pulled taut. The door to the office slowly creaked open and Sly was jerked off the bookshelf. As he flew out the window, he saw Bentley holding tightly to the other end of the string. Murray pedaled fast as he pulled them away from the building.

"Whoa!" Sly yelled as he flew through the air.

Murray pulled them across the playground and down the hill. Soon, they were out of sight of the schoolhouse. But they were picking up speed!

"B–B–Bentley!" Murray yelled. "How do you make this thing stop?!"

"I would recommend using the brakes," Bentley replied. The little turtle tumbled about inside the wagon. "But unfortunately I haven't installed any yet. That was going to be my project for next week!"

At that, the tricycle slammed into a large oak tree. Sly let go of the cup-municator and flew through the air. Murray somersaulted over him and tumbled across the grass. Bentley pulled his arms, legs, and head into his shell and ejected from the wagon. He skipped across the ground before spinning to a stop.

"I'm sorry, guys," Murray said as he stood and dusted himself off. "Are you okay?" he asked his friends.

Sly looked around and saw that everyone was all right. "It looks like we're just fine," he replied. "Man, are we lucky!"

Bentley stood and adjusted his thick glasses. "Lucky?" he asked. "We just crashed and failed our mission!"

"Well, we definitely crashed." Sly took off his hat. "But we didn't fail our mission." He held out his hat to show that it was full of delicious cookies. "Dig in, fellas!"

"Yahoo!" yelled Bentley and Murray.

The three friends sat under the tree and ate their prize. After his second cookie, Sly smiled at his best friends. "This must *be the sweetest-tasting failed mission ever, huh, guys?"*

Their mouths full, Bentley and Murray simply nodded in agreement.

Back in Monaco, the full-grown Sly Cooper smiled at the memory. That night, under that big oak tree, the world's greatest band of thieves had been born.

Murray gave the large statue a final shove. With a *THUD*, it slid the rest of the way into the van. Sly leaped from the roof, ripping off the borrowed guard uniform and hat in midair. "Great job, guys," he said as he landed. "The statue is ours!" He placed his blue hat back onto his head. "Now that's what I call teamwork!"

"Uh, Sly," came Bentley's voice. "I think we have a problem."

Sly peered inside the open van. Just past the large statue, Bentley sat in the middle of the command center. He was surrounded by all kinds of high-tech electronic equipment, including a state-of-the-art surveillance system, a slew of super–spy gadgets, and several advanced computer workstations. Bentley pointed to the simplest device in the van — a clock.

"We ran twelve minutes and thirty-seven seconds over schedule," Bentley reported.

"Ouch," Sly replied. "So that means . . . uh . . . what does that mean?"

"I'll tell you what it means!" Bentley squirmed in his seat. "It means that we missed our boat out of here!" The little turtle rummaged through a stack of paper on the control console. He finally pulled out the boat schedule and squinted at it. "And the next boat doesn't leave for forty-five minutes!"

"Forty-five minutes?" Murray echoed. He raised his chubby hands to his head. "Oh, no! Inspector Fox will catch us for sure! What are we going to do?"

"Don't worry, boys." Sly smiled and twirled his cane. "I can keep the nice inspector busy until we leave."

He bounded toward a nearby drainpipe, placing his cane in his mouth as he climbed toward the roof.

"Forty-five minutes, Sly!" Bentley reminded him. "Forty-five minutes!"

CHAPTER 10

Inspector Carmelita Fox stood outside of Madame D'Oinkeau's mansion. All the guests had gone and the grounds were dark. Carmelita still wore her black evening gown, but she had slipped her brown leather jacket and tan gloves on over it. She aimed a flashlight at the ground with one hand. She held a small tape recorder in the other.

"Suspect, Sly Cooper, entered the building from the rooftop," she dictated into the recorder. "It appears he entered through the skylight."

The inspector walked around the back of the mansion. She came upon a set of stairs leading into the ground. They stopped at the basement door. Her flashlight beam washed over fresh footprints emerging from the top of the steps. They led away from the mansion and into the darkness.

Carmelita switched on the recorder. "It appears that Cooper exited through the basement." She noticed another set of footprints. "Cooper always works with a team of two other thieves. All are experts in the field." The second set of prints was much larger. "It appears as if the one called Murray helped him carry out the statues," she dictated, a note of triumph in her voice.

Inspector Fox followed the trail to a dingy alleyway nearby. The footprints led to tire tracks, which she traced out from between the buildings toward a small stone bridge.

"Tire tracks confirm a getaway vehicle," she reported into the microphone.

"The suspects appear to be headed toward the waterfront."

Carmelita followed the tracks to the middle of the bridge. The trail vanished where the hard cobblestones began. She knew they had crossed the bridge, heading for the docks. But they could have turned down any street along the way. She had lost their trail.

"*Wow*, he's good," she said to herself. "It's a shame he's not working for the police."

"Now why would I want to do that?" asked a voice from behind her. "I'm having so much fun as a thief, and I really don't like doughnuts!"

Inspector Fox spun around. No one was there. Then she looked up. "Cooper!" she shouted. Sly Cooper sat perched atop a lamppost.

"Inspector Fox," said the thief. "We really need to stop meeting like this." The raccoon smiled and launched himself off the lamppost. He spun in midair and landed silently on the cobblestones below.

Carmelita's heart raced. She gazed into Cooper's eyes and for a moment was captured by the raccoon's handsome smile. Then she shook her head and reached into her leather jacket. She whipped out a large walkie-talkie. All she had to do was press the TRANSMIT button and call for backup. She had teams of Interpol officers combing the streets looking for Cooper and his band of thieves. One call, and they would all race to her location. Then she would finally nab the infamous Sly Cooper.

The raccoon twirled his cane, then swung it toward her. Carmelita ducked, but instead of hitting her head, the cane knocked the radio from her hand. It flew through the air and slid across the stones on the far side of the bridge. "There's no need for that, Ms. Fox," he said.

Carmelita lunged forward and grabbed his cane. She pulled him close. "Listen, you ring-tailed rat," she growled.

"Who do you think you are? And who do you think you're dealing with?!" His grin widened and her grip tightened. "This isn't some kind of game," she yelled. "And you're not going to get away this time!"

Inspector Fox stared into his eyes a bit longer. Then she growled and pushed him away in frustration. Sly brushed off his shirt, then casually leaned against his cane.

"You know I only steal from master thieves," he announced. "I never take anything from the hard-working citizens you love so well." Sly pushed his hat back on his head. "So, when you think about it, we're kind of on the same team — without the doughnuts of course."

"Don't get me started," yelled the inspector. "Where do you think those other thieves get their loot?" She pushed a finger onto his chest. "They steal it! So I don't care where you think you sit on the thief food-chain. You're still breaking the law!"

Sly sighed and strolled to the bridge

railing. "Do you remember the first time we met?" he asked, casually changing the subject. "At the opera?"

Carmelita crossed her arms and narrowed her eyes. "How can I forget?"

Sly chuckled. "Yes, I do like to leave an impression." The raccoon leaned on the railing and peered toward the river. "You were pretty unforgettable yourself that night." Sly turned to face her. He stretched both arms across the railing and leaned back. "And could we have asked for a better place for a first rendezvous? Paris: the City of Lights!"

Carmelita laughed. "City of Lights? You were lurking in the shadows, looking for your next prize to steal."

Inspector Fox thought back to when she first met Sly Cooper. She remembered him as a burglar with clumsy tools and ragged clothes. Of course, her memory could have been exaggerating things a bit.

"On the contrary, my dear Inspector,"

Sly challenged. "I was out enjoying the night air."

Carmelita laughed. "Try your smooth-talking charm on someone else, Cooper," she retorted. "You were on the roof of the Paris Opera House that night. And you were up to no good."

Sly's jaw dropped. "Me? Up to no good?" He placed a hand on his chest and smirked. "Why, I was merely taking in the fine architecture."

"You were planning how you were going to rob the opera house blind!" Carmelita's smile was gone. She tightened her lips. "It was the biggest night of my career and you almost ruined it!"

CHAPTER 11

Sly sighed. Carmelita Fox looked especially pretty when she was angry. He watched as she blew a strand of hair out of her face.

"I remember that night well," he said. Sly pictured himself leaping gracefully across the Parisian rooftops toward the opera house. "I had snuck into the Paris Opera House and saw a lovely young police officer on the stage."

Carmelita joined Sly at the railing. "It was my first chance to prove myself to Inspector Barkley. I had to show that I had what it took to take over the department."

She gazed out over the river. "All I had to do was secure the Paris Opera House and protect the Diva Diamond. Then Barkley could retire happily, knowing he had made the right choice."

Sly pictured the scene in his head. The short badger didn't seem very happy with Carmelita that night. The two of them stood on the stage next to the lead actress, a large elephant named Madame Tuskinanny.

"You better be up to the job, Fox!" shouted Inspector Barkley. Even though Sly was hiding in the balcony, he could hear every word. The angry badger pointed to the pink diamond around the elephant's neck. "If anything happens to this diamond, you can kiss your career good-bye!" he shouted.

The short badger and the elephant stormed off the stage. Carmelita Fox stood alone in the spotlight. Sly felt sorry for the attractive young police officer. He had planned to snatch the diamond away from Madame Tuskinanny, who had come to own the diamond under questionable circumstances herself. But perhaps he would skip this one. After all, he didn't want to get the young officer in trouble.

The raccoon climbed out of a window and crawled up a narrow drainpipe. He hopped onto the opera house roof and looked out at the beautiful city. As he stood near the ledge, he pulled out his map. Maybe he could steal from another master criminal that evening.

Just then, the door to the roof slammed open. Carmelita Fox emerged, eyes ablaze. "Freeze, criminal!" she yelled. "What are you doing up here?" A stream of police officers poured from the door behind her. The large gorillas quickly surrounded Sly Cooper.

"Wait a minute," said Carmelita. Sly was pulled from his memory. They were back in Monaco, back on the bridge. Carmelita was back to pointing and scowling at him. "I brought you down single handedly, Cooper!"

"Are you kidding?" asked Sly. "It took at least —" He thought for a moment. "— ten . . . no, *twenty* of your goons to take me down." He laughed. "And really, I just let them catch me just so I could meet you."

"You're amazing." Carmelita's expression softened. "You're starting to believe your own lies."

"No lies," said Sly. A grin stretched across his face. "It's not every day I meet a beautiful, smart, and talented fox like you."

Carmelita looked away. He could tell she was a little embarrassed. Then she turned back and glared at him. "If you really wanted to meet me, then why did you escape and make me look like an idiot in front of my boss?"

Sly winced as he remembered what happened next. Carmelita had tied him up and hidden him away in the janitor's supply closet. She planned to keep him there until the show ended later that night.

"I got lucky," Sly replied. "The janitor happened to let me out."

"Do you have any idea how much trouble you got me into?" asked Carmelita.

"Yes, I do," he replied. "That's why I tried to help."

Sly pictured himself back in Paris, inside the opera house, locked in the janitor's closet. Carmelita had bound him tightly with a thick rope. But how was she to know that she wasn't tying up any ordinary thief. No mere ropes would hold a *master* thief. Sly had quickly cut them. However, a locked closet door was a different matter. Luckily, the janitor arrived to take care of that.

⌣   ⌣   ⌣

"Hey!" the janitor yelled as Sly popped out of the tiny closet.

"Thanks for the help, pal," said Sly. He darted past the old dog and leaped into the air. "And you're doing a fine job here. Everything is very . . . clean!"

Sly grabbed a nearby rope and swung his cane. The hook sliced through the rope, and a heavy sandbag fell toward the floor. Holding the opposite end of the rope, Sly was hoisted into the air. He let go of the rope and soared toward the catwalks. He landed gracefully on the rickety framework hanging over the stage.

The cunning raccoon had dashed out of sight just in time. Inspector Barkley, Carmelita, and Madame Tuskinanny ran into view. They headed straight for the open closet door.

The short badger picked up a piece of cut rope. He waved it over his head. "So where is your thief, Ms. Fox?"

"He was here a minute ago," Carmelita stammered.

Barkley pointed to the empty closet. He trembled with anger. "And what kind of police officer stashes a crook in a janitor's closet?!" The short badger pushed his face close to hers. "Perhaps I was wrong about you," he growled. "If you can't handle a single petty criminal, how can you be head of the entire department?"

Petty criminal? *Sly thought.* There's no need for name calling!

Madame Tuskinanny put a hand on her pink diamond. "Now that there's a thief on the loose, I'd better put the Diva Diamond in my safe!" she said, frowning at Carmelita. Then she stormed off, the ground shaking with each step.

"I'd better go, too," Inspector Barkley added. "Someone has to protect that diamond."

Sly watched as Carmelita hung her head. She turned on her flashlight and looked for clues around the closet door. But Sly knew she wouldn't find any.

The young police officer continued her investigation around the rest of the stage area. Creeping along the catwalks above, Sly Cooper followed her. He watched silently as she interviewed employees and searched everywhere for some sign of the missing thief.

Sly sighed. He felt sorry for Carmelita Fox. He could always turn himself in. That would certainly help her. Then again, no self respecting master thief would simply turn himself in. There had to be a better way.

Sly crouched on the catwalk, lost in thought. Carmelita turned a corner and walked out of sight. Sly was about to follow her when he saw Madame Tuskinanny's dressing room door open. He expected to see the large elephant. Instead, out stepped the show's stage manager, Pierre. The short aardvark poked his head out and suspiciously looked around. When he was sure the coast was clear, he crept from the dressing room. In his hand was the Diva Diamond. The stage manager was stealing it for himself!

Pierre ducked around some flat

scenery pieces and out of sight. Sly sprung into action. He leaped to another catwalk and then soared into the air, flipping and landing silently on the stage below. He hid behind another flat set piece. With his cane at the ready, he listened for the stage manager. As the aardvark's footsteps grew louder, Sly held out his cane.

Sly chuckled. "Watch your step!"

The thief tripped and landed with a THUD! as Sly caught the diamond in midair. Pierre was out cold.

CHAPTER 12

A shrill scream trumpeted throughout the theater. Hiding near the side of the stage, Sly watched as Madame Tuskinanny charged onto the main stage. Inspector Barkley followed her closely. The two found Carmelita in the center of the stage. Barkley rounded on Officer Fox.

"Carmelita Montoya Fox!" yelled Barkley. "First you lose the thief and then you lose the diamond!" The inspector shook more than ever. He looked as if he might explode at any moment.

"Excuse me?" asked Carmelita.

"It's horrible!" wailed Tuskinanny.

"The show will start soon and I can't perform like this!"

"This is the worst foul up in police history," Barkley yelled.

Sly watched as the two continued to yell at Carmelita. Once again, he felt sorry for the young officer but not for long. Using his cane, he cut through the rope holding his special package. *What opera is complete without a surprise ending? Sly thought.*

Suddenly, a dark figure dropped onto the stage from above. Carmelita, Inspector Barkley, and Madame Tuskinanny dove out of the way. The figure hit the stage with a loud WHAP!

"Hope you like your care package, Ms. Fox," Sly whispered. "Special delivery, just for you."

Sly watched as Carmelita stepped closer to the figure. He was tied with rope and had a paper sack over his head. She removed the sack, revealing Pierre, the *stage manager. Hung around his neck was the Diva Diamond.*

"Pierre!" cried Tuskinanny. "He stole the diamond?" The diva rocked back and forth, almost fainting.

Madame Tuskinanny shook her fist at the criminal. "I trust you, Pierre!" she shouted. "You've betrayed me."

Inspector Barkley grabbed Carmelita's hand. "Great job, Fox!" he said. He shook her hand vigorously. "Or I should say, Inspector Fox!"

Madame Tuskinanny took back the diamond, and Barkley led away Pierre. Sly looked on as Carmelita remained on the stage. He watched as she reached into the paper sack and pulled out a small, folded piece of paper. It was cut in the shape of a raccoon's head.

"I'll never forget the look on your face when you first saw my calling card," said Sly. Back on the bridge, he grinned at Inspector Fox. "It was priceless. Your expression was torn between love and anger." He sighed dramatically and peered out over the water. "I'll never forget it. So innocent. So cute."

"Innocent and cute?!" Carmelita growled. "Don't even think of talking down to me, Cooper!"

"I just call it like I see it," Sly replied with a smug grin. "And what I saw that night was a real hero. Well, thanks to me, of course."

"Times have changed," said the inspector sharply. "I'm not the same naïve rookie you first met." At that moment, she dove across the bridge, somersaulted, and grabbed the walkie-talkie from the ground. "All officers, move in on my position!" she shouted into the radio.

"Yes, ma'am," replied a crackled voice. Several sirens wailed from the streets around them.

Carmelita stood and smiled triumphantly. "You're going to look great in stripes, Ring-tail!"

The sirens grew louder, but Sly didn't look worried. He returned her smile and hopped onto the railing, spreading his arms. "It's time to go, Inspector."

"But you can't swim!" Carmelita's eyes widened. "You'll drown!"

"That's true," he replied. "The only water I like is in a cup. But then again, what's a poor raccoon to do?" He leaned back and fell off the bridge.

"No!" she yelled.

Sly tucked in his legs, flipped in midair, then landed solidly on both feet on the deck of a boat. Beside him were Murray, Bentley, and their getaway van.

Inspector Fox leaned over the railing. Sly could see relief in her eyes. But as Sly watched, the relief quickly changed into blazing anger.

"I'll get you, raccoon!" she bellowed. "Mark my words. I'm going to get you!"

Sly waved. "I'll miss you, too, Carmelita!"

Sly thought he was lucky to be chased

by someone like her. Maybe, someday, she would actually catch Sly Cooper, the master thief of all thieves. Until then, she would have to settle for capturing the heart of a thief.